MAX AND KATIE'S
WILD WEST ADVENTURE

BY SAMANTHA METCALF

ILLUSTRATED BY IAN R. WARD

Published in Great Britain in 2016 by:
Mysteries in Time Limited
info@mysteriesintime.co.uk

Illustrated by Ian R. Ward.
www.ianrward.co.uk

A catalogue record for this book is available from the British Library.

ISBN 978-0-9935660-4-2

Hi! I'm Katie and I am 8 years old. Max is my older brother. He's really clever. He helps me with my home work when I'm stuck. He knows everything! But don't tell him I said that. He can get really annoying and know-it-all. He is always telling me stuff, but sometimes it's just too much. All I want is a simple answer, like 'yes' or 'no'. Instead, it's always 'maybe, because...' So annoying.

But he's not so bad. He always looks out for me. And we have fun playing games together.

I think my favourite thing is playing outside in any weather! I love going to the park, especially the adventure playground with the huge, curly slide. You can go really fast on that one, especially when you lie down! Mum hates it when I come home covered in mud, but I can't help it. The fun parts of the park are always the muddiest.

Hey, I'm Max and I'm 11. I love reading. I read comics and cartoons that make me laugh, and I read adventure stories about knights and castles, or pirates and buried treasure! Mum is always telling me I have an overactive imagination. I can't help it. My mind just starts picturing loads of weird stuff.

I also love solving puzzles. Grandpa always buys me books full of word-searches and crosswords. I like to time myself and see how fast I can solve them.

Katie is my younger sister. She is really energetic and fun to be around. She's really fast and sporty. I wish I could be as good as her at sports. But don't tell her I said that. She can also be really annoying, when she can't sit still for more than five minutes. And she doesn't stop talking!

But she's cool. I'm pleased she's my sister.

1

"Why do you always have to be SO annoying?" grumbled Max.

Katie ignored him. She was concentrating on perfecting her horse impression. She was trotting up and down the living room, round and round the coffee table. She had set up little obstacles, which she leapt over and landed with a shake of her mane.

"Neigh!" she said, as she scraped at the floor with her right leg. She was getting ready for her biggest jump yet: the large stool next to the armchair. She took a deep breath, then ran towards it.

She must have jumped too soon, because her trailing leg hit the edge of the coffee table and she tumbled to a stop on the armchair, giggling and out of breath.

Max was definitely not laughing with her. Katie's leg had knocked the coffee table, sending his house of cards tumbling to the table-top in a jumbled mess.

"Now look what you've done!" shouted Max. "I

spent ages building that! I was onto my third layer, which was a record for me!"

"Sorry Max," said Katie, suddenly feeling guilty.

Max had been working really hard to perfect his card tricks all weekend. Although the tricks very rarely worked, he was getting really good at building towers from cards. But she didn't have time to tell him.

"Look what the postman brought!" called Mum from the doorway.

It was another adventure.

Max quickly collected up all of the playing cards and shoved them messily into the card box, while Katie took the turquoise time machine from Mum's arms.

Upstairs, they settled into their usual places on the carpet in Max's bedroom and opened the box.

Where would their next adventure take them?

Mission Plan

Place: American Wild West
Date: 1867

The American Wild West was full of adventurous
people hoping to make their fortune. Most
prospected for gold, opened saloons or became
cowboys looking after cattle on ranches.

However, some people turned to crime. Near
the town of Redwood, there was a series of
stage coach robberies. Masked gunmen held up
stage coaches in the middle of the desert,
and stole the hard-earned money of innocent
people. So far, nobody had been hurt. But it
was just a matter of time before one of the
robbers used their pistols.

Task:

Can you help the sheriff catch the stage
coach robbers before somebody gets hurt?

2

"Yee-ha!" cried Max happily. "I've always wanted to meet a real-life cowboy!"

Katie agreed. She loved cartoons with cowboys, because that meant horses too!

They were both so excited about this adventure, that they jumped up, called out to their mum where they were going, then went straight to their grandfather's fancy dress shop.

"Hi Grandpa," said Max, waving. "We've got a party to go to and we want to go as cowboys."

"Er, cowboy and cowgirl," corrected Katie.

Grandpa peered over the top of his glasses. "Oh?" he said suspiciously. "Whose birthday is it?"

"Er, I don't think you know him," replied Max. "No, I'm sure you don't. Just someone from school."

Grandpa nodded. "I think we have some good Wild West costumes here," he said. "Follow me."

Max and Katie followed him to the other side of the shop, where there was a whole row of cowboy costumes. Katie immediately picked out a bright pink hat with sequins on the wide brim.

She was admiring her reflection with this sparkly hat on, when Grandpa spoke to her very seriously.

"That's a fun hat for a party," he started, "but if you want to really look the part, this hat is much more realistic."

He held up a dark brown hat made from soft suede. Katie frowned at it, looked back at the pink hat in the mirror, then back to the brown hat.

Unhappily, she took the pink hat off her head and held it out towards her grandfather, who did the same. But Katie didn't let go. Even when Grandpa pulled the sparkly hat towards him, Katie was still clutching it.

"Katie?" said Max with a warning tone. "Grandpa's right. You should look the part for real."

Katie sighed loudly. "OK, OK, you win." She let go and took the realistic hat with a scowl.

They picked out a long skirt for Katie, with a waistcoat over a white shirt and a green kerchief tied loosely round her neck. Max wore chaps over his own blue jeans and a waistcoat over a checked shirt. He wore cowboy boots and a red kerchief.

Their grandfather stepped back and smiled at them. "You really look the part now!"

Max stood in front of the mirror. "This town ain't big enough for the both of us," he said to his

reflection. He was talking with a drawl out of the corner of his mouth.

"Why are you being so weird?" asked Katie, still grumpy about the hat. "You're looking in a mirror. That's your reflection. There's only one of you!"

Grandpa smiled. "It's a line from a famous cowboy film," he explained. "He's getting into character."

"Ah, I see," she said, watching Max with interest.

Max walked with a swagger round the room. Katie copied everything he was doing, and they were both soon giggling together.

"Thanks Grandpa!" they both called out.

They dipped their cowboy hats to him and swaggered out of the shop. They stayed in character all the way home.

Once they were home, they called out to Mum to tell her they were back. Then they sneaked upstairs so she wouldn't see them in their Wild West clothes. They didn't want to tell any more lies.

3

Upstairs, they opened the history book and learnt all about the Wild West, or the American Frontier as it was also called. They read about the Gold Rush, the Pony Express, outlaws and Native Americans.

"It seems like a dangerous, lawless place, where everyone carried a gun," said Katie.

"Don't worry," replied Max. "We're going back to a time when they had sheriffs to uphold the law."

Max passed Katie the Time Travel Sticker.

"A horse-shoe! Horse shoes are lucky!" said Katie happily. "Maybe we'll be fine after all!"

They were ready to go.

Max pushed the button on the time machine.

4

The room swirled around them and they saw flashes of light as they travelled through time.

They landed with a splash on a muddy street with people busily going about their lives. There were wooden buildings with wide, covered porches along both sides of the road, with horses tied to the wooden fence posts.

Max and Katie looked around. A stage coach pulled by horses had stopped outside a hotel. Suitcases were being unloaded and carried inside.

Suddenly, a loud noise erupted nearby. They followed the noise to the swing-doors of a saloon. They crouched down and ducked their heads so they could see what was happening inside.

There were two men sitting at a table playing cards. One was dressed like a cowboy with a moustache. A large crowd was watching.

"This is your last chance," snarled the cowboy. "If you lose this next game, your horse is mine."

The man opposite him was dressed very smartly, with his shirt sleeves rolled up to his elbows. He looked very nervous; he had beads of sweat on his forehead.

Max and Katie watched the next round of the card game with interest. The saloon was now silent. Everyone was hoping the smartly-dressed man would win. When he turned his cards over, the whole room cheered. His cards were high!

5

The cowboy raised his right hand to silence everyone. He looked surprisingly calm.

Everyone held their breath as he turned over his own cards. Just as he did so, Max saw the cards change. He had swapped them. He had cards up his sleeve. He was cheating! Nobody else would have seen it. Max only saw because he was crouched down, so his eyes were level with the man's sleeves.

He had to help! But what could he do?

Max didn't stop to think. He stood up and swung the doors open with force. Everyone inside the saloon stopped and stared at him. But he forgot the doors would swing back and they hit him in the face! Katie stifled a giggle.

Max swallowed his embarrassment and tried again, this time ready to catch the doors. He was inside now. There was no going back.

6

Max gulped.

He was going to announce what had happened, but he spotted the extra cards fall expertly from the cowboy's sleeves into the up-turned hat of his passing friend. There was no proof! It would be Max's word against this cowboy's.

He had to think fast.

"Howdy," he said, dipping his hat to the room. "I have an offer for you," he said to the cowboy. "Double or quits. I will let you shuffle the deck of cards, I will then let you pick any card. If I can guess your card, then you have to give this man's horse back to him."

There was a gasp from the crowd of people watching. The cowboy stroked his moustache while watching Max for what felt like an eternity.

"And if you get it wrong?" he snarled.

"Then you double your winnings; you not only keep his horse, but you get my horse too," said Max confidently.

Katie threw her hands to her head. His *horse*?! HIS horse?! What horse?! She groaned to herself. This could end very, very badly.

Max may know a few card tricks, but there's no way he could magic a horse from thin air.

7

To Katie's dismay, the cowboy agreed.

Max stepped forward, rolled up his sleeves and insisted the cowboy do the same. Max then pulled out his own deck of cards from his pocket. He shuffled them by cascading them from left to right like a fountain. He was enjoying the attention. Katie knew he was showing off now.

Katie could see that the people watching were very impressed with his shuffling skills.

The cowboy's moustache twitched as he watched.

Max gave the deck of cards to the cowboy and asked him to shuffle them. The cowboy did so slowly and carefully, then followed Max's instructions and put them face down on the table.

"Now please cut the deck three times," said Max. The cowboy did so, by picking up the top half, setting down on the table, then picking up the remaining cards and putting them back on top. Each time, he was left with a single pile of cards in a different order.

"Are you confident that the cards are well-shuffled?" asked Max.

The cowboy's lip curled up into a snarl. Max took this to mean 'yes' and continued.

He picked up the deck of cards. Keeping them face down, he fanned them out in front of the cowboy.

"Pick a card, any card," he said. "Take a look and show it to everyone here, but don't let me see it. Then place it on top of the deck face down."

Katie watched the cowboy do as he was asked.

"Now cut the deck three more times," said Max.

The cowboy did so, then sat back and folded his arms. "Are you ready to lose your horse, stranger?" he growled at Max.

Katie couldn't watch. Max had tried this same

trick on her five times this weekend. It had never worked. Something always went wrong. This was a bad idea. She started looking around the busy streets for an escape route.

Max turned the deck of cards over on the table so they were face up. He fanned them out for everyone to see. He looked the cowboy in the eye and hoped his nerves were hidden. He picked up a single card.

"Is this your card?" he asked, holding up the seven of diamonds.

8

Katie held her breath.

The room erupted into a sudden cheer. Katie looked back inside the room and saw Max being hugged by the man whose horse was now safe.

"Thank you so much," he said. "This saloon and my horse are the only things in this world that I own. My name's John. If there's anything I can do to repay you, then just ask."

The whole crowd was happy. Max was a hero!

Angrily, the cowboy stood up tall. He knocked into the table, sending cards flying everywhere. There was a sudden loud bang as the table fell with a crash to the floor. The cowboy towered over everyone in the room, especially Max.

He was scowling at Max. "This is not over," he growled. "You haven't seen the last of me."

Katie stumbled back just in time, because the

cowboy threw the saloon doors open and stormed out into the street. His spurs sounded with every angry step, followed closely by his two worried-looking friends.

Katie joined Max inside. People were taking turns to shake his hand and pat him on the back. Katie rolled her eyes; she'd never hear the end of this. She pulled Max outside into the fresh air.

"What were you thinking?!" she hissed at him. "That trick never goes right - do you realise what could have happened?!"

"But it DID work!" he laughed.

Katie was about to argue back, when she was interrupted by the sound of hooves thundering past. The angry cowboy and his gang galloped past on their way out of town. The horses kicked mud up all around, covering Max and Katie from head to foot!

They looked at each other and giggled.

9

Just then, the sheriff came out of the saloon and introduced himself. He saw their muddy faces and smiled. "Come with me, we'll get you cleaned up!"

They followed him across the muddy street. Katie saw several men wearing big boots who were loading their horses with strange-looking tools.

"What do they need pickaxes and sieves for?" whispered Katie when the sheriff was out of earshot.

"They are prospecting for gold," explained Max. "They search the countryside, especially the rivers and streams. If they see anything golden, they scrape at rocks with the pickaxe or sift through the dirt with the pan. Anything tiny falls through but any larger nuggets are caught in the pan, like a sieve."

Katie liked the idea of looking for gold.

Within a few steps, they were inside the jailhouse. This single room doubled up as the jail and the sheriff's office. There were wanted posters on the walls. Katie especially liked the look of one of the criminals: it was a sketch of a man's face, but his hat was pulled low and his kerchief was pulled over his nose and mouth.

"How can anyone recognise this person from this sketch?!" laughed Katie. "You can only see his eyes!"

The sheriff looked very serious. "It's all we've ever seen of the Stage Coach Robber. He has been a menace to people arriving into this town."

The sheriff brought them a bowl of water and a

towel to clean the mud from their faces.

"You were very brave back there," he said to Max.

"Or stupid," grumbled Katie under her breath.

"I have been looking for a deputy," said the sheriff. "Someone who is brave and honest and willing to stand up to bullies. Are you interested?"

Max grinned as the sheriff gave him the badge. "Howdy! Deputy Max at your service," he said.

The sheriff smiled. "It suits you!"

Just then, there was the sound of hooves outside.

"That must be my family!" said the sheriff, standing up. "They are on their way from the East. Their stage coach should be arriving today."

He went to the door and scanned the street for his family. He stopped and waited, frowning.

A single messenger jumped down from his horse and raced up the steps with his hat in his hands.

"Sheriff, it's your family," he said seriously. "There's been another robbery."

10

The sheriff had many questions, most of which went unanswered.

"Don't worry, your family is safe," said the messenger.

The sheriff introduced the messenger to Max and Katie.

"This is Emmett," he said. "He runs the town's first telegraph company."

After greeting Max and Katie, Emmett gave the telegraph that he had received to the sheriff. "It happened about two hours ago. They were shaken up, but not hurt. They have stopped in the next town and they will finish their journey after a short rest, when they feel up to it. That's all we know for now."

The sheriff thanked the messenger, who nodded, turned and left.

"We should wait until my family has arrived and

settled in comfortably, then we'll ride out to the site this afternoon," announced the sheriff. "Maybe we can set up an ambush and catch these robbers once and for all."

Max and Katie looked at each other.

"Er, ride?" asked Max.

"Yes," replied the sheriff. "Is that a problem?"

Katie interrupted. "No, no problem at all!"

Katie dragged Max outside, where she explained her plan. "Don't worry, it's easy! We have at least two hours until we need to leave. I can teach you how to ride a horse!"

Max looked unsure, but he nodded in agreement.

"But I can't ride a horse in this skirt," said Katie. "And I will fall off if I try to sit side-saddle like ladies are supposed to!"

"But girls can't wear trousers in the 1860s," replied Max.

"I know. I have a plan."

11

They went to the saloon to find John.

"We need your help!" said Max.

"Anything for you," he replied. "I'll be honoured to repay you for your kindness this morning."

John rummaged through a drawer and gave Katie what she needed: a pair of scissors, a needle and some thread. He showed her to an empty hotel room, where Katie locked the door and got to work.

She took her skirt off and cut from the hem towards the waist. She then did the same at the back. Next, she sewed the front and back together at the left, then the same on the right. She held up her creation: they looked like very wide trousers. It was just like the split skirts that would soon become fashionable for cowgirls.

She put the skirt back on, and looked in the mirror. She was very pleased with herself, because you couldn't tell! It still looked like a skirt when she

walked normally, but she could now sit on a horse

properly, with one leg on each side.

She hoped Grandpa wouldn't be too cross with her.

12

Meanwhile, John took Max to his stable behind the saloon, where he got his horse saddled up.

"My sister wants to learn how to ride a horse," lied Max, as John fastened the saddle onto the horse.

John smiled as he handed the reins over to Max. "Good luck!"

Just then, Katie joined them. They thanked John, waited for him to leave, then they got to work.

When they were definitely alone, Katie showed Max how to get on a horse. Unfortunately, when he tried it for the first time, he somehow used the wrong foot and ended up sitting the wrong way round!

They both collapsed into giggles, because he was facing the horse's tail. Max had to duck when the horse twitched its tail so hard that it nearly hit him in the face!

They worked hard for the next two hours. Katie taught Max how to walk, trot, canter and - most importantly - how to stop.

Max knew he wasn't an expert, but at least now he knew how to hang on and pretend!

13

Just as they were finishing, they heard a commotion out in the street. They heard thundering hooves coming to a stop and loud voices. They went to investigate.

The cowboy from the saloon had just arrived on his horse.

"It's the Indians," he announced. "They are to blame for the attack on your family's stage coach."

The sheriff was watching the cowboy closely. "And what makes you say this?" he asked.

"They were seen in the area," he replied, still on horseback. "It has to be them."

By now, a crowd had gathered around the horses. People were talking amongst themselves and the noise was getting louder, angrier.

"Let's go find them and teach them a lesson!" yelled one man, shaking his fist in the air.

There was a general murmur of agreement, and the sheriff had to shout out to be heard.

"Stop!" he yelled. "There will be NO retaliation without knowing the facts." He glared round at the crowd. "We will wait until my family arrives this afternoon with the full story of what happened. And then - and only then - will myself and my deputy investigate. Is that understood?"

Everyone was watching the sheriff silently. It felt like time had stood still. The wind swirled around their legs and blew balls of tumbleweed along the road. The atmosphere was tense.

Slowly, one by one, the crowd started to leave in different directions, murmuring to themselves.

14

Suddenly, something caught their eye.

"The stage coach!" cried Katie eagerly. "Let's go!"

The sun was shining as the stage coach arrived into town. People were standing on their porches watching the new arrivals with interest. Suitcases were unloaded and carried to the sheriff's home.

The sheriff had a big smile on his face as he held his hand out to help a lady in a beautiful dress step down from the stage coach. She wore a long dress with a bustle at the back. It was navy blue with white lace on the cuffs. Her wavy hair was pinned up under a small hat with a lace veil.

They hugged each other, then laughed as a small boy jumped down into the sheriff's arms.

The sheriff introduced his wife and son to Max and Katie.

"Mary and Billy, please meet Deputy Max and

his sister, Katie," he said.

Once they had all greeted each other, the sheriff led them to the jailhouse for some lunch.

After lunch, the sheriff got straight to the topic of the robbery.

"Tell me everything," he said. "Don't leave anything out, no matter how small or unimportant you think it is."

15

"Well, we were travelling quite quickly across the plains," started Mary. "Soon, it was desert on all sides, except for some large balancing boulders and an enormous cactus plant that looked like a person waving his arm. The coach stopped abruptly and the horses reared up on their back legs, distressed."

"What did you see when you looked out of the window?" asked the sheriff.

"There was a bandit on either side of the coach with pistols pointed at us," she continued.

"Did you see their faces?" asked Max.

"No, they were wearing kerchiefs over their noses and mouths. All we could see were their eyes."

Billy's eyes were wide and sparkling. "Maybe it was the Sundance Kid or Butch Cassidy or Jesse James or Billy the Kid!" he suggested excitedly.

The sheriff smiled at his son. "No, no, I don't

think so. Those outlaws prefer robbing trains or banks." He turned back to Mary. "A local cowboy has been spreading the rumour that the Indians were to blame," he asked. "Could this be true?"

"Definitely not!" replied Mary. "It was the Indians who came and scared the bandits away! If it hadn't been for them, we would have lost everything!"

"What were the robbers wearing?" asked Katie.

"Well, the leader was wearing a checked shirt and a dark hat," explained Mary. "Similar to Max here."

Everyone looked at Max.

"Er, it wasn't me, I pr-promise!" stuttered Max.

The sheriff smiled. "Don't worry Max, I trust you." He was quiet for a short while, before hitting the table with his fist. "We have to stop these robbers. We cannot let them terrorise our roads."

"We have to catch them red-handed," said Max.

Katie agreed. "Max is right. We should set a trap."

"But there's only one of me," said the sheriff in

despair. "I can't surround a gang of robbers by myself, and I can't trust anyone else to just arrest them! Anything could happen."

Max cleared his throat. "Er, you're not on your own," he said. "You have your deputy!"

Everyone looked at Max, who felt like he was shrinking under their gazes. He knew he had to be strong. He sat up straight.

"Yes," agreed Katie. "I'll help too. What do you need us to do?"

"Are you sure?" asked the sheriff. "I thought you weren't happy about riding out when I asked earlier."

"Us? Not happy about riding? Ha!" replied Max, perhaps with too much enthusiasm. "It's OK now, because I taught Katie how to ride this afternoon."

Katie fought the urge to correct him, and smiled through gritted teeth.

Together, they hatched a plan.

16

The sheriff spent some time teaching Max some cowboy skills that might come in useful.

"I used to be a cowboy on a ranch," explained the sheriff. "I had to round up stray cattle like this."

He showed him how to lasso an object with a rope. It was harder than it looked. On the first attempt, Max twirled the rope around his head but forgot to throw it, so he ended up roping himself.

The second attempt went better, but he forgot to keep hold of the end of the rope. He spun it around his head, then threw it towards the target, but the end of the rope slipped through his fingers and away.

Other attempts simply didn't hit the target. He didn't feel ready, but it was time to leave.

The sheriff packed a saddle bag with everything they would need.

The sheriff's family waved them off as the sheriff,

Max and Katie set off on horseback. Max was riding John's horse and Katie had borrowed a horse from the sheriff.

Katie ignored the strange looks from the townsfolk as she rode past. They passed many ladies on horseback, but they were always sitting side-saddle. They gasped when they saw Katie riding with one leg on each side of the horse.

They looked shocked but excited by the idea of a split skirt allowing Katie to ride like a man.

17

The sun was beating down on them and it wasn't long before the muddy path was replaced with the dusty red sand of the desert. The horses kicked up the dust and sand into their faces, so they pulled their kerchiefs over their noses.

Along the way, they passed large groups of men laying tracks through the desert. They were singing as they worked, laying the tracks in a straight line.

"They have a long way to go!" commented Katie, looking out to the distant horizon.

In the distance, they saw a train of covered wagons, probably families on their way to find a new life in the West. They were travelling in rows, kicking up dust storms across the desert.

After about an hour of riding, they reached the place where the robbery had happened.

"There's the balanced boulder on the hill," said

Katie, pointing at the rocks on the cliff above.

"And here's the cactus that's shaped like someone waving!" added Max. The cactus was taller than Max and had one branch reaching upwards.

They were in the right place.

The sheriff talked through the plan one last time.

"Any questions?" he asked.

Max and Katie shook their heads.

"We're ready," said Max.

The sheriff nodded, then turned his horse.

"Yah!" he shouted to urge his horse on faster. The sheriff then galloped off into the distance in a cloud of swirling dust.

Soon, except for the distant cawing of the circling vultures, there was silence. Max and Katie looked at each other uneasily. They were on their own.

To pass the time, Katie lay on her back and watched the clouds move across the sky.

Their horses were tied up in the shade of the

boulders, resting.

"Look at that cloud there," she said to Max. "It looks just like a rabbit!"

"A very odd-looking rabbit with a long tail and a beak!" laughed Max, watching the wind blow the clouds across the sky.

They scanned the horizon for new movement. Max leapt up in excitement and pointed to the right.

"Look!" he cried out and pointed to the distance. "There's a herd of wild bison!"

"What on earth is a wild bison?" asked Katie.

"They are better known as buffalo," said Max. "They are huge animals that were hunted for their meat, fur and skin. We're lucky to see them!"

Katie didn't respond, because something had caught her eye.

There was a steady dust cloud that appeared to be moving, growing. It was getting closer.

Someone was getting closer.

18

Max and Katie spread out. Max hid behind the boulders, while Katie hid on the other side of the road, behind the enormous cactus.

They heard the rhythmic hooves of the horses that were pulling the stage coach.

They knew they had to wait. They had to wait and see if the robbers turned up. They also had to wait until they heard the signal, but they were both feeling nervous.

What if the robbers knew they were there?

They could be in terrible danger.

The stage coach slowed a little as it approached the boulders.

Max and Katie waited.

Max was holding his breath.

Katie's hands were shaking.

19

Suddenly, the stage coach horses stopped in their tracks and reared up on their hind legs. They were snorting noisily.

"Woah, calm down," soothed the driver of the stage coach as he pulled back on the reins.

The horses didn't respond though; they were still uneasy about something nearby.

Max and Katie didn't have to wait very long, because three riders came thundering along the path towards the stage coach. They all wore cowboy hats and kerchiefs, so all you could see was their eyes.

They quickly surrounded the stage coach, waving their guns.

"We don't mean you any harm, we just need your money and your jewellery," shouted the leader in a gruff voice. "Pass it out and we will let you be on your way."

There was no response from inside the coach, so he indicated for one of the other robbers to investigate. The closest cowboy rode his horse alongside the coach. He leaned in towards the window and looked confused.

"What on earth...?" he started, then leaned closer to make sense of what he could see.

The sheriff was inside the coach, but he was dressed as a lady, pretending to sleep in the corner.

As the man leaned in, the sheriff jumped up quick as a flash to grab the robber's arm. He quickly handcuffed him with an expert movement.

"Now!" he shouted to Max.

Max already had his lasso in his hands. He edged his horse slowly forwards, then started to swing the rope around his head, the way the sheriff had taught him today. This was more difficult than it looked. When practising, he had missed the target more times than he hit it! But now he only had one chance.

"Here goes!" he thought to himself.

He gave the rope one final swing and let go of the last bit of slack; the rope was at its longest now. Max let go and watched the lasso fly through the air towards the nearest gunman.

Luckily, the man had his back to Max and had no warning that the rope was flying towards him. Max felt like it was all happening in slow motion, because he had time to realise that the rope was slipping too fast through his fingers.

He grabbed at the end, just in time! Max watched the lasso fall down around the cowboy, and he pulled the rope to tighten it around the robber's arms.

Max was so excited, that he cheered, forgetting that there was still another armed robber very close to him!

Max quickly jumped down from his horse and tied the end of the rope to the nearest boulder.

The lead robber looked from the first robber who was handcuffed, to the other one who had been roped. He realised this was an ambush and that he was now outnumbered.

He kicked his horse with his sharp spurs and turned quickly to escape.

Katie knew the sheriff and Max were both busy. She was the only one left to chase him.

It was up to her now.

20

Katie signalled for her horse to walk. She navigated expertly round the cactus plants and then gave chase. She was leaning down low to the horse's neck for balance as they started to go even faster.

They had moved from a canter into a gallop and Katie was enjoying the rush of wind past her ears. The robber up ahead now realised that Katie was chasing him; he kept turning his head to check how close she was.

He tried everything to shake her off. He rode his horse through some arches made of rock, hoping the low ceilings would slow her down. He forgot that Katie was a lot shorter than him, so it was much easier for her to duck down. This didn't slow her down at all.

Katie soon settled into the stride again, urging her horse on. She couldn't let him get away!

They had left the flat desert behind and were now moving towards a rocky area with some trees dotted around.

Katie followed, closing the gap. There were lots of little obstacles here that Katie guided the horse over.

"I wish my horse-riding teacher could see me now!" she thought to herself, smiling.

Up ahead, it looked like it was a dead end. The horse ahead slowed down as the robber looked around for another way out. There was none. He kicked his horse hard and headed for the only escape: over a large fallen tree.

Katie knew this was the only way to chase him, but the jump was bigger than anything she had ever tried before. She almost turned away, but stopped herself. She could do this!

She got her horse in position and they were off.

They picked up speed quickly and at the right moment, Katie signalled for the horse to jump.

Soon they were flying! Katie couldn't believe it! They landed smoothly on the other side and spotted the robber ahead. They thundered onwards. She was catching up!

Soon, there really was a dead end. They both slowed down and were now facing each other. It was only now that Katie realised how far they had ridden, how far away Max and the sheriff were. She also realised that this man had a weapon; Katie didn't.

He must have realised the same thing at the same time, because Katie could see his eyes smile. He pulled his pistol from his holster and slowly raised it. Katie was looking down the barrel of the gun.

Everything else blurred together.

It felt like time stopped.

21

Just when Katie thought she was out of options, the robber's face drained of colour. He dropped the pistol and raised his arms in a surrender gesture.

Katie didn't understand until she looked behind her. There, standing in a semi-circle around them, were at least twenty Native Americans, all with their bows raised and pointing their poised arrows at him.

The chief approached Katie and bowed his head to her.

"Hello, Katie," he said kindly. "You are very brave, and an excellent horse-rider!"

Katie was stunned. "H-h-how do you know my name?"

The chief smiled. "The sheriff visited us this morning after he left you at the boulders," he said. "He explained everything and asked for our help."

Katie was very grateful and thanked him.

She turned to the masked bandit, whose kerchief had slipped down. She could see his face, but it wasn't the cowboy she had expected to see.

"John?" she asked. "John, is that you?"

John lowered his eyes in shame. "Yes Katie, I'm very sorry."

"But why? I can't believe you would do something like this."

"It is hard making a living in this place," he

explained. "I struggle to pay the bills and could be homeless soon. I see that cowboy swagger round town, taking what he wants. I know he was cheating in that game, but I had no choice. But I promise you I have never hurt anyone. I don't even have any bullets in my pistol!"

Katie felt sad for John.

"I must say though Katie," he continued. "You really have learnt to ride a horse like an expert in just a few hours!"

22

The chief and a couple of his men escorted Katie and John back to where Max and the sheriff were waiting. Katie giggled when she saw the sheriff, because he was still wearing his disguise!

Max grinned when he saw his sister.

"Here she is, the Hero Horse Rider of the West!" he said.

"And here's the Lasso King!" laughed Katie.

They all returned to town, where the sheriff locked up the three robbers.

"What will happen to John and his two friends?" asked Max.

The sheriff sighed. "Well, John was telling the truth about their pistols: not a single bullet between them," he explained. "So I think the law will be softer on them. They may do some time in prison, but they will be free in the not-too-distant future."

23

The first thing the sheriff did, after he had changed out of the dress, was call a town meeting.

People were shocked to see the sheriff standing side-by-side with the Native American chief.

"You caught him then," shouted one man.

"Why isn't he in jail, where he belongs?" yelled another.

The sheriff raised his hands to quieten the crowd and started to talk. He explained what had happened.

"Without their help, we would have lost the real thief. Tonight, we will have a party to celebrate," he said, turning to the chief. "And we would like you to be our guest of honour."

The crowd murmured amongst themselves, but slowly, one by one, they started to approach the chief to shake his hand.

Even the cowboy from the saloon shook his hand. "I am sorry," he said, removing his hat. "I blamed you when you were really our friend."

The chief smiled. "Friends," he agreed.

Everyone set to work setting up bales of hay and bringing out tables and chairs from their houses. It wasn't long before a bonfire was lit and a band was playing. People were dancing and laughing into the night.

24

Max and Katie were sad to leave, but they said their goodbyes and stepped back into the shadows. The sound of the banjos and the harmonicas hung in the air as they felt time spinning around them.

Back safely in Max's bedroom, Max and Katie felt really proud of themselves. They had both shown real bravery.

"Thanks for teaching me how to ride!" said Max.

"You're welcome. You were pretty good at it," replied Katie. "Hey, do you think you could teach me how to do that card trick? It was great seeing that cowboy's face! Nobody knew how you did it!"

Surprised, Max pulled out his deck of cards and started to teach Katie. He wondered how soon his sister's impatience would surface and she would get bored and give up.

It only took ten minutes.

The End.

See you on our next adventure!